Copyright © 2005 by Ken Brown

The rights of Ken Brown to be identified as the author and illustrator of this work
have been asserted by him in accordance with the Copyright, Designs and Patents Act, 1988.
First published in Great Britain in 2005 by Andersen Press Ltd., 20 Vauxhall Bridge Road, London SW1V 2SA.
Published in Australia by Random House Australia Pty., 20 Alfred Street, Milsons Point, Sydney, NSW 2061.
All rights reserved. Colour separated in Switzerland by Photolitho AG, Zürich.
Printed and bound in Italy by Grafiche AZ, Verona.

10   9   8   7   6   5   4   3   2   1

British Library Cataloguing in Publication Data available.

ISBN 0 86264 875 0

This book has been printed on acid-free paper

MONSTER
Mucky Pup

Written and illustrated by
Ken Brown

Andersen Press
London

Mucky Pup had chased things all morning.
He'd chased a fly . . .

He'd chased the leaves . . .

He'd even chased his tail . . .

But now he was bored with chasing things.
Then he saw that the shed door was open.
"That looks more fun," thought Mucky Pup . . .

And indeed it was . . .

. . . but it would be even more fun with two.
So Mucky Pup set off to find his friend, Pig, to join in.

"Hello, Hen," said Mucky Pup. "Have you seen Pig?"
But Hen just shrieked and flew away!
"She's very unfriendly," thought Mucky Pup,
puzzled. "How strange!"

"Hello, Cat," said Mucky Pup. "Have you seen Pig?"
But Cat just yowled and fled across the farmyard!
"And *she's* even more unfriendly than usual,"
thought Mucky Pup.

"Hello, Duck," said Mucky Pup. "Have you seen Pig?"
But Duck just leapt off her nest into the water, quacking loudly!
"Now that really is odd," thought Mucky Pup.

"Hello, Donkey," said Mucky Pup. "Have you seen Pig?"
But Donkey brayed in a panic, kicked up his heels
and galloped away across the field.
"What is *wrong* with everybody?"
thought Mucky Pup.

HEEEE-
Haaaww!

HEEEE-
Haaaww!

"Hello, Goat," called Mucky Pup. "Have you seen . . . ?"

But before he could finish, Goat lowered his head and charged across the orchard towards him. This time it was Mucky Pup's turn to run, and run he did — as fast as he could, across the field and through the hedge to safety!

As he was catching his breath, he heard a familiar voice:
"Hello, Mucky Pup!"

"PIG!" gasped Mucky Pup. "Am I glad to see you!
All the animals have gone mad. They've all run away from me
except Goat, and he chased me across the orchard!"

"I'm not surprised," said Pig. "Just come over here, and look at yourself in the stream!"
Mucky Pup looked. He got such a fright . . .

. . . that he grabbed hold of Pig!

They overbalanced and splashed into the stream . . .

. . . and that really was fun!

"MUCKY PUP, MUCKY PUP!"
"Uh-oh," said Pig. "They're calling you. Time to go!"

"Oh, what a mess!"
they heard the farmer's
wife exclaim . . .

"Well you can't blame Mucky Pup
this time," said the children.
"Just look how clean he is!
Come on, Mucky Pup,
say goodbye to Pig.
It's time for tea!"